Jim Bridger's
Alarm Clock

and Other Tall Tales

for Henriette

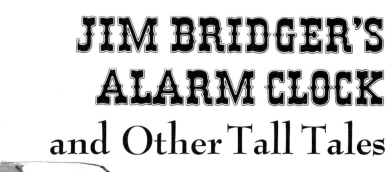

JIM BRIDGER'S ALARM CLOCK
and Other Tall Tales

by Sid Fleischman

illustrated by
Eric von Schmidt

A Unicorn Book
E. P. Dutton   New York

Library of Congress Cataloging in Publication Data

Fleischman, Albert Sidney.
Jim Bridger's alarm clock and other tall tales.

SUMMARY: Three tall tales about Jim Bridger and
several of his unbelievable discoveries in the
wilderness of the West.

1. Bridger, James, 1804–1881—Juvenile fiction.
[1. Bridger, James, 1804–1881—Fiction. 2. Western stories.
3. Humorous stories] I. von Schmidt, Eric. II. Title.
PZ7.F5992Jg [Fic] 78-5854 ISBN: 0-525-32795-9

Published in the United States by E. P. Dutton, a Division
of Sequoia-Elsevier Publishing Company, Inc., New York
Published simultaneously in Canada by Clarke,
Irwin & Company Limited, Toronto and Vancouver

Editor: Emilie McLeod

Printed in the U.S.A. First Edition
10 9 8 7 6 5 4 3 2

Contents

Jim Bridger's
Alarm Clock

Jim Bridger was a mighty tall man. When he stubbed his big toe, it took six minutes before he felt it and yelled "Ouch." But he's not famous for being tall.

Jim Bridger was a long-haired mountain man. In fringed buckskins and Indian moccasins, he wandered through the wilderness of the Old West before almost anyone else. It was Jim who brushed the hair out of his eyes and first discovered the Great Salt Lake. They

4

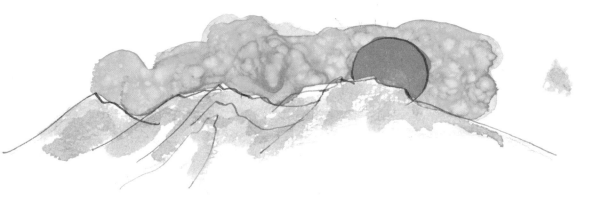

might have named it after him, but no one believed he'd found water you couldn't sink in. Jim shrugged his big, bony shoulders and headed back to the mountains.

One day his horse broke three front teeth grazing on a patch of green grass. That's how Jim discovered a petrified forest. The grass and trees had turned to stone for miles around. "Petrified, all petrified," he

reported when he got back to civilization. "The bees and the wild flowers, and yes sir, some of those trees had petrified birds on their limbs singing petrified songs."

6

But he's not famous for all those things.

Jim Bridger was a ramshackle, sharp-eyed army scout. In time they named a fort and a forest after him, and a pass and a creek and a mountain or two.

He once pointed to a mountain in the distance, flat-topped and red as a Navajo blanket. "Stranger," he said. Jim liked to talk to strangers; they were so few and far between in the wilderness. "Stranger, look how that mountain has grown! When I first came out here, it was nothing but a red anthill."

And that's what Jim Bridger's famous for. That mountain. He made an alarm clock out of it.

The way it happened, Jim was out in the wilderness, as usual, when a blizzard whipped down out of Canada. His beard froze. The fringe in his buckskins froze. And his long hair hung like icicles. Then a spark from his campfire lit inside his moccasin. That spark was so cold it frostbit him, and Jim decided it was time to seek himself a warmer climate. He headed south.

9

He traveled through the snow for days and nights. He didn't dare to stop and rest. He knew a man could sleep himself to death in the blizzard and bitter cold.

Jim was all tuckered out and knew he couldn't go much further. Then, through the chill daylight, he caught sight of that red, flat-topped mountain in the distance. It was slab-sided, too, and he had bounced echoes off it many a time. He reckoned from where he now stood, it would take about eight hours for an echo to return.

Jim Bridger gave a yip of joy and made camp. He laid out his bedroll on the snow. Then he gave an ear-quivering yell.

10

"WAKE UP! WAKE UP, JIM BRIDGER, YOU
FROSTBIT, NO-ACCOUNT RASCAL!"

Then he climbed into his bedroll, clamped his eyes
shut and fell away to snoring. Oh, he snored thunder-
bolts, and dreamed of hot biscuits and gravy.

Exactly seven hours and fifty-six minutes later, Jim
Bridger's Alarm Clock went off.

11

"WAKE UP!" roared the echo. "WAKE UP, JIM BRIDGER, YOU FROSTBIT, NO-ACCOUNT LIAR!"

Jim roused from his bedroll, all refreshed and feeling strong as a new rope. It was a week before he reached Fort Bridger, where the sun was shining and no one believed his story.

But a trapper came straggling in and said, "It's true, every cussed word. I found the coals of Jim's campfire and bundled up in furs to catch some shut-eye. Next thing I knew, that mountain commenced booming. I didn't get a wink of sleep. Doggonit, Jim, you snore loud enough to drive pigs to market!"

14

The Fiddler
Who Wouldn't Fiddle

Jim Bridger was coming back from exploring Yellowstone Park when he bumped into a brand-new town. It stood smack-dab on the spot where he'd camped the day of the big blizzard. But folks didn't know he'd been there first, so they didn't name the place after him. They called it Blue Horizon.

Blue Horizon didn't amount to much, but it did have a general store, a stable, a blacksmith, seven saloons and a funeral parlor.

Jim said his howdys, but everyone he met had the grumbles. Sitting around the stove in the general store, he tried to cheer them up by reporting the wonders he'd seen in the Yellowstone.

"Durn my gizzard if steaming water didn't shoot up out of the earth red-hot from hell. And boiling water flows out of the rocks into the prettiest lake full of trout you ever saw."

"Can't no trout live in boiling water," grumbled the mayor, chewing a cigar as if it were beef jerky.

"You're exactly right," Jim answered. "Down below, the water's cold as a frog. The hot spring floats on top. Oh, I ate a mess of trout and never once had to build a cook fire and get out my skillet."

"You eat your fish raw?" the blacksmith asked.

Jim shook his head. "No, sir. It was just a matter of hauling up that trout slowlike through the boiling top water. When I unhooked it, the trout was cooked and ready to eat."

18

The mayor kept chomping his cigar. Jim could see nobody gave a hoot about his hot-and-cold lake. They didn't even accuse him of lying.

"Something bothering you gents?" he asked.

The mayor nodded. "We got to call off the barn dance tonight. The fiddler won't fiddle."

Now Jim Bridger loved a frolic, and it had been a long time since he'd kicked his heels to a jolly tune.

"Who's the fiddler?" he asked.

"Buryin' John Potter, the undertaker. He's hornet-mad because folks didn't elect him mayor instead of me."

The more Jim Bridger thought about it, the more his feet hankered for fiddle music. So he sauntered across the street to the undertaker's parlor.

"You can't fool me, Buryin' John Potter," said Jim. "I see your fiddle on the wall, but that don't mean you can play a note. On purpose, I mean."

"Can, but won't," grumbled the undertaker. He was hollow-cheeked, sharp-chinned and long in the arms. Wearing his black claw-hammer coat, he looked like a crow, except that he chewed tobacco.

"No, sir," Jim said. "If you was to saw your fiddling bow across those catgut strings, I'll wager you couldn't hit two notes out of five."

"Haw," said the undertaker, smirking.

"Reckon you don't even know 'Chicken in the Bread Tray Pickin' Up Dough.' "

"By heart," said the undertaker sourly. "But I ain't fiddlin' tonight. Don't think you can sweet-word me into changing my mind."

"Wouldn't think of it," Jim replied. "But I'm a powerful fine judge of fiddle music. Once heard Jingle-Bob Earl play a frolic back in Missouri, and I guess you'll agree he's the mightiest fiddler who ever was."

"Faw," snorted Buryin' John Potter. "He couldn't play high C if he was standing on a stepladder. I'm the mightiest fiddler who ever was—but I ain't fiddlin' tonight."

And Jim said, "I brought a gourd plugged full of hot steam from the Yellowstone, and it's still perishin' hot. That Yellowstone steam takes years to cool off. I figured to use that gourd as a foot warmer—the nights are turning chilly already, wouldn't you say? Buryin' John, that Yellowstone foot warmer is yours

if you can play the screech box half as clever as Jingle-Bob Earl. Come outside and prove it."

The undertaker took down his fiddle, and the two men rode out to a distant spot west of town. Buryin' John tuned his strings, clamped his sharp jaw on the edge of the fiddle box and began beating time with one foot as if he were pounding a stake into the ground. He spit tobacco juice and ripped out "Turkey in the Straw."

Jim thought he'd never heard it played so sweet, but he said, "Won't do. Jingle-Bob Earl played louder'n that. His fiddling rattled windows for miles around. Do you know 'Scooping Up Pawpaws'? Or 'Have You Seen My New Shoes'?"

"Both," Buryin' John muttered, and commenced sawing away twice as loud as before. The music raised the sap in Jim's feet. It was all he could do to keep from leaping to his heels and raising dust.

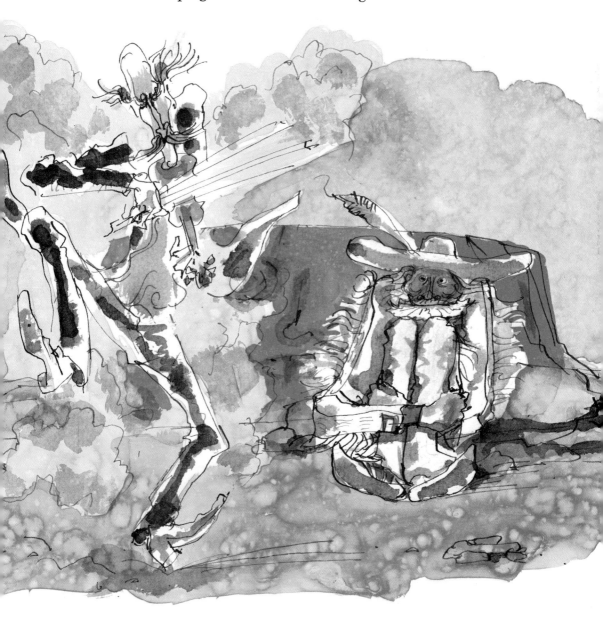

Then the undertaker lifted his chin from the fiddle and shot tobacco juice to one side. "Reckon that gourd foot warmer is mine," he declared.

"Not so hasty," said Jim. "You call that a contest? Why, Jingle-Bob Earl could fiddle all night without playing the same tune twice."

The undertaker rosined his horsetail bow, tucked the fiddle back under his jaw and scraped away. Hour after hour the bow cut wild figures in the air. Now and then Buryin' John squirted tobacco juice without missing a note. Jim had never heard such jimber-armed fiddling. It was an ear-quivering wonder.

Finally the sun began to dive for home. Jim jumped up, stomped his feet to the music and sang out.

> You could fiddle down a possum from
>   a mile-high tree,
> You could fiddle up a whale from the bottom
>   of the sea!

And he said, "Buryin' John, you win! You're the mightiest fiddler that ever was! The Yellowstone foot warmer is yours."

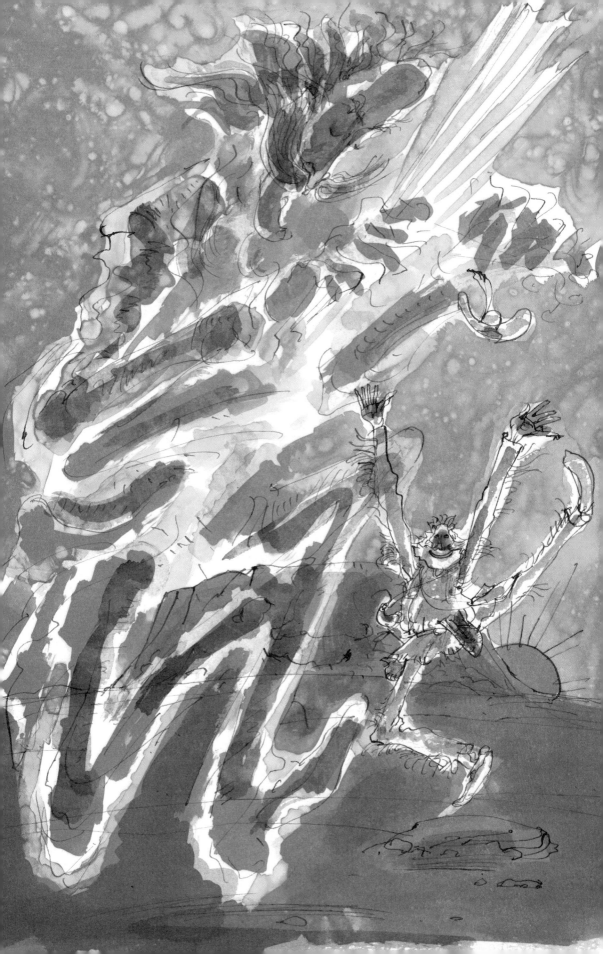

When Jim got back to the general store, it was falling dark. "Grab your women and head for the barn!" he exclaimed. "The frolic's about to commence."

The barn filled up in no time. Folks stood around waiting for Buryin' John. They'd heard him practicing his fiddle all day long. A mule began to bray, but they couldn't dance to that. Dogs began to bark, but they couldn't dance to that.

Finally, the mayor, who was there to do the fiddle calling, said, "Can't be a frolic without a fiddler. We might as well go home."

"Keep your hair on, Mayor, and the barn doors open. All the windows, too," said Jim, cupping an ear. "Coming this way is the grandest, mightiest fiddling you ever heard. Caller, clear your throat!"

26

Suddenly, bounding back from Jim's slab-sided echo mountain, came the first notes of "Turkey in the Straw." So taken by surprise were the folks in the barn that they stood frozen like bird dogs on point.

Then Jim leaped to the center of the floor with hours of stored-up frolic in his feet. He kicked his heels and the dance was on. The fiddle caller aired his lungs.

Grab your partners, make a square,
Music's comin' from I don't know where!

The rafters shook with a romping and a stomping,
and the barn was aswirl with calico skirts. The mayor
shucked his coat and kept calling.

> Dive for the oyster,
> Dig for the clam.
> Dive for the sardine,
> Take a full can.

Suddenly the undertaker, in his black claw-hammer coat, loomed up in the doorway. When he saw all the jollification, the wad of tobacco jumped out of his mouth.

"Durn my gizzard, if it ain't Buryin' John!" Jim called out.

"That's my fiddlin'!"

"Oh, you're a sly one." Jim laughed, thinking fast. "That was eternally clever of you to echo your fiddling so you could kick your heels to your own music. Had everybody fooled, you did! They thought you were hornet-mad. Don't stand there stiff as a crowbar. Grab a partner, Buryin' John, and lift your hooves to the mightiest fiddler that ever was."

The Fifth of July

Jim Bridger had just discovered an invisible mountain
and hankered to tell someone about it. So he headed
out of the wilderness and back toward civilization.

35

It was high summer when he rode into Blue Horizon, and dusk was settling over the streets. The place had grown to a flea-hopping city since the last time Jim had come along. There was a bank on the corner, a jailhouse across the way, three churches and a hotel with rocking chairs on the front porch. A bugle band was playing, too, and Jim thought at first they were playing to welcome him back.

He stood on the hotel porch, whipped off his hat and said, "I'm mighty obliged, folks, and eternally, dog-eared honored. Now let me tell you about the most amazing place I just discovered. . . ."

But no one paid any more attention to him than to a barnyard rooster. The band marched away, leaving him standing. Jim went looking for his old friends, but they had moved away. The streets were full of strangers.

So Jim turned to a couple of cowboys trying to ride their horses into a saloon. "Hold on, gents," he said. "You might not believe this, but I discovered . . ."

Before Jim could finish his sentence, the cowboys began yipping and yapping and hollering like coyotes. They drew their guns and commenced shooting at the moon, which hadn't risen yet.

A man in a black come-to-Jesus coat came along, and Jim figured him for a preacher. "Reverend," the mountain man said, "let me tell you how I discovered . . ."

"Amen," said the preacher with a hasty smile. "I'm late for the church supper and pie-eating contest." And Jim was left standing again.

Now that the first stars were out, men were shooting off pistols, rifles and shotguns. Even the sheriff was blazing away. They all appeared to be trying to puncture new holes in the sky.

Out in the center of the street, a blacksmith lifted one anvil on top of another, wedged a stick of dynamite between them and yelled "Stand back!"

The sheriff lit the fuse and the explosion boomed like a cannon shot. It tossed the top anvil, somersaulting it through the air. That was so much fun they did it again.

Jim was about to leave town in a hurry, when he ran into a beaver trapper he'd known up on the Wind River.

"Shoeless Ed!" Jim exclaimed. "I can't calculate what's got into these folks, but let me tell you about . . ."

"I don't go by the monicker of Shoeless Ed Kitchen anymore, Jim. Ain't respectable for a judge. Folks call me Your Honor. And you're just in time!"

"For what, Your Honor?"

"Jim, you've been in the wilderness too long. Why, it's the Fourth of July! We been celebratin' all day—

sack races and heaps of food and tugs-of-war. The sheriff wouldn't allow the boys to shoot off their guns until sundown. And the sun's down!"

With all the racket going on, Jim figured he'd never get anyone to listen to how he discovered an invisible mountain. So he joined in the celebration. He gave a yip of his own and began firing his long-barreled musket.

Blue Horizon didn't quiet down until the last lead ball was shot skyward, the last ounce of gunpowder was used up and the last stick of dynamite popped the anvil into somersaults. There was nothing left to do but go to sleep.

Jim slept on a pile of hay in the livery barn, and dreamed of his invisible mountain. He was brought

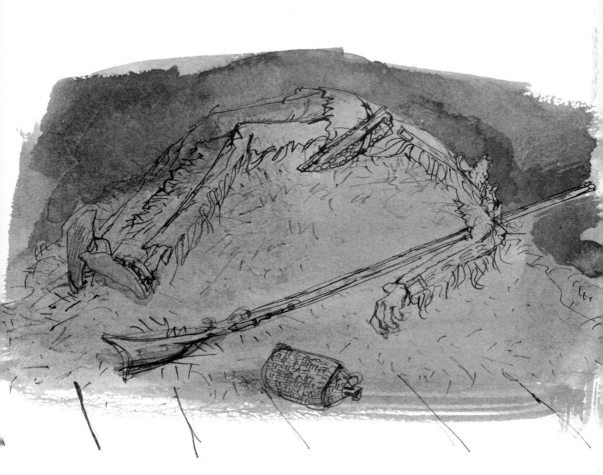

awake by the clatter of horses' hooves. He heard loud
voices and the breaking of window glass.

Jim ambled outside to see what mischief was afoot.
The morning dark had not yet lifted, but Jim could
make out the shapes of six men entering the bank
through the shattered windows.

A seventh man, slim as a toothpick, sat waiting on

his horse. "Blow up the safe and throw out the money bags, boys," he hollered. "No rush about it. These here city folks don't have the brains of a turkey buzzard."

Jim rushed back to load his musket, only to remember he'd used up his lead and powder. "Cuss me for a turkey buzzard," he groaned.

47

The sheriff had been roused from his sleep too, and
His Honor turned up looking sallow and sag-faced. He
had the stomach miseries from the pie-eating contest.

"Top o' the mornin' to you, gentlemen," said the
outlaw.

"It's Seldom-Seen-Slim," muttered the sheriff.

And His Honor bellowed, "Well, don't stand there
like a mule, Sheriff. Start shootin'!"

"Haw-hee-haw!" laughed Seldom-Seen-Slim. "You
folks did all your gun shootin' yesterday. Welcome to
watch us rob your bank, gents. Reckon it an honor.
I ain't often seen."

48

Dawn came up like a prairie fire, and money bags came flying out the broken bank windows.

The sheriff suffered in silence, gritting his teeth, gaps and all.

Jim shrugged his shoulders and said, "Seldom-Seen-Slim, I don't suppose you'd care to hear about the invisible mountain I discovered?"

"Time to ride!" the outlaw called to his men.

"Well, I wouldn't ride south," Jim said. "Nobody knows this country better'n I do. You'll run into petrified grass, and your horses'll bust their teeth. Up north you'll come to a river so devilish twisty and crooked, ever' time you cross it you'll end up back on the same side. Head east is my advice."

"Don't think you can trick me so easy," remarked Seldom-Seen-Slim. "Sun'll be in our eyes."

The gang galloped out of town due west, and Jim grinned.

His Honor's stomach rumbled. "Sheriff," he said. "Get up a posse quick. Blast that pie-eating contest! I feel like I swallowed a full-grown bear, claws and all."

The sheriff's face was red with outrage and embarrassment. He hitched up his empty gun belt. "You want us to chase them with clubs, Your Honor?"

"Won't need a posse," Jim said. "Open your jailhouse. Seldom-Seen-Slim and his gang'll be right back. Now, about that invisible mountain. You see, I caught sight of a jackrabbit grazing about twenty yards off. Biggest I ever saw. The pelt alone would cover a parlor floor. I'm partial to rabbit stew so I raised my musket. Well, the boom of the gun didn't so much as lift the rabbit's ears. I couldn't have missed a gnat at that distance, but I missed that rabbit. I tried again and again, but that infernal rabbit just went on munching grass. So I reckoned I'd catch it with my bare hands. I ran for it and charged smack into an invisible mountain. I tell you, that mountain was pure glass.

50

Clearer'n a windowpane. Not only that, it was one-
hundred percent pure *magnifying* glass. Why, that
was nothing but a little bunny jackrabbit munching
grass—a full fifty miles away."

Right then there came a zinging and whining of
bullets from the west, and Seldom-Seen-Slim and his
gang came galloping back to Blue Horizon.

"Quick, Sheriff!" hollered Seldom-Seen-Slim.
"Take these bank bags and lock us up! The whole
U.S. Cavalry is after us! Hear that? Hear them bugles
blaring and rifles shooting and cannons going off? We
give up! Lock us up before they fill our hides with
lead!"

"There's the jailhouse, gents. Step right in," Jim
said, and the sheriff locked the door on them.

54

Jim decided it was time to move on. No telling what other wonders were out in the wilderness to be discovered. But he paused to listen to the bugle band and the wild, ear-quivering rumpus echoing off his blanket-red, alarm clock mountain on the Fifth of July.

About the book

"Jim Bridger was a mighty tall man. When he stubbed his big toe, it took six minutes before he felt it and yelled 'Ouch.' "

So Sid Fleischman begins his comic saga about the legendary mountain man who discovered Great Salt Lake, a petrified forest where petrified birds sang petrified songs—and most important, a flat-topped mountain he used as an alarm clock.

SID FLEISCHMAN believes in laughter. His novels *Chancy and the Grand Rascal* and *Jingo Django*; the McBroom tall tales; and his shorter books, *The Ghost on Saturday Night* and *Me and the Man on the Moon-eyed Horse*, are guaranteed to make readers laugh and deeply care about the characters who live in them. He is a screenwriter and professional magician.

ERIC VON SCHMIDT has done dozens of lively drawings to match the high-spirited humor of *Jim Bridger's Alarm Clock*. He is the illustrator of Sid Fleischman's novels, as well as books of his own. A painter and a folksinger, he lives in New Hampshire and Florida.

The display types are Comstock Lode and Bernhard Modern. The text type is linotype Bodoni Book. The two-color art was prepared in pen and ink with wash and reproduced as dropout halftones. The book was printed at Rae Publishing Company, Inc.

56